can't catch Me!

Constanze
von Kitzing

Barefoot Books
step inside a story

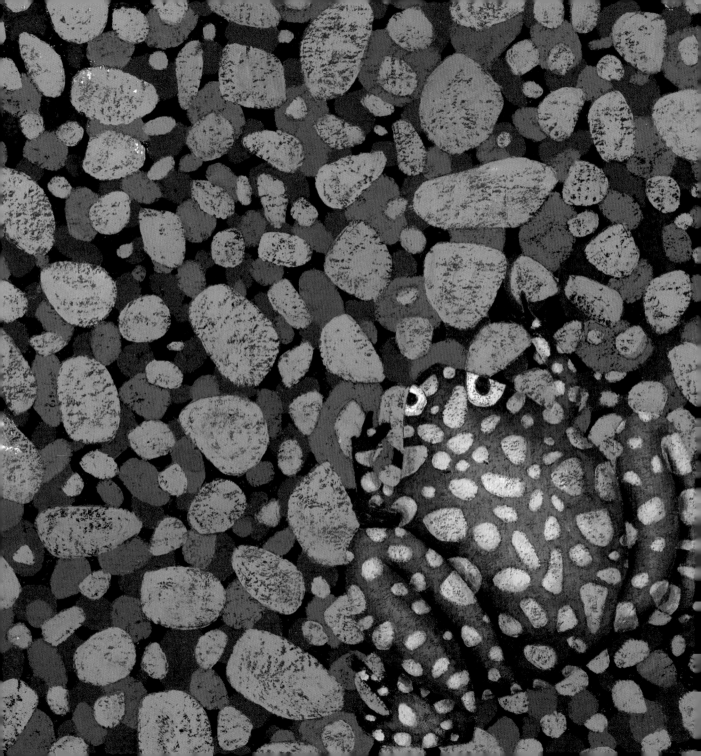

"I'm going to catch you!" Said Little Lion.

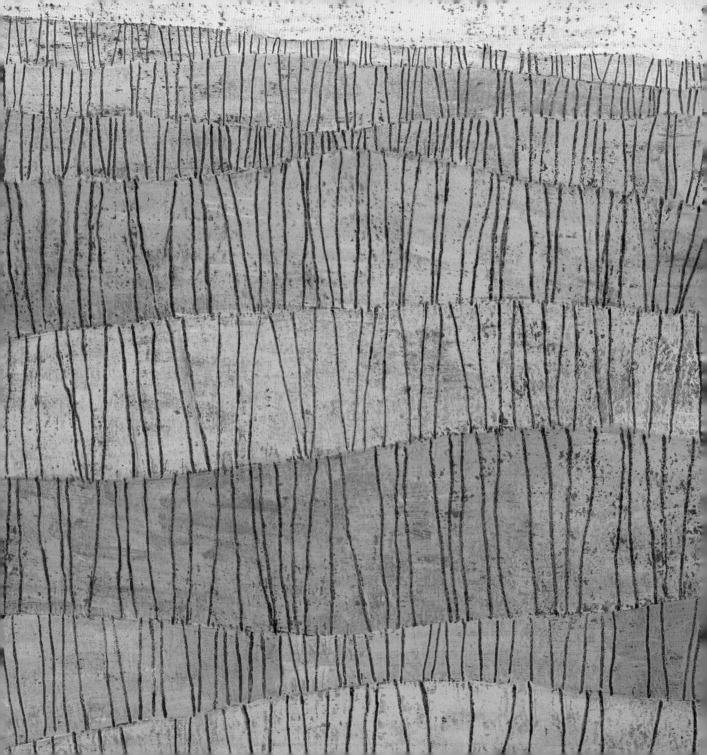

"No, you won't!" replied the grasshopper.

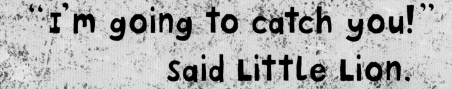

"I'm going to catch you!"
Said Little Lion.

"NO, you won't!"
replied the **bird**.

"I'm going to
catch you!"
      Said Little Lion.

"No, you won't!"
replied the rabbit.

"I'm going to catch you!"
Said Little Lion.

"NO, you won't!" replied the **zebra**.

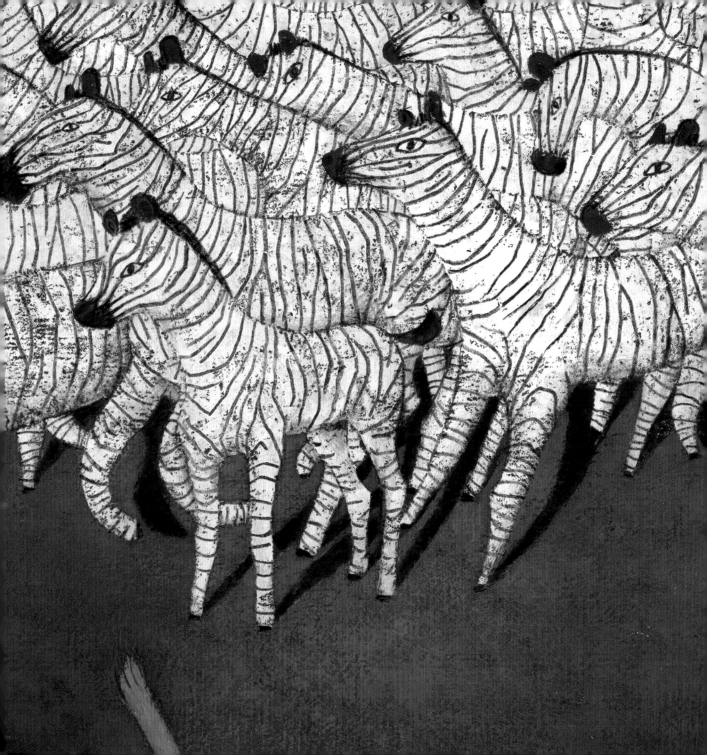

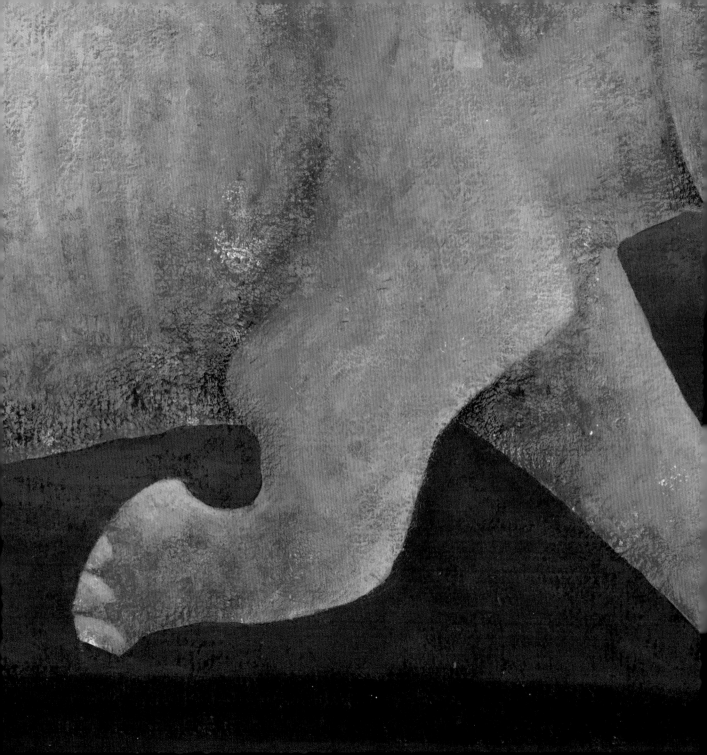

"I'm going to catch **YOU!**" roared the **rhinoceros.**

"No, you won't!"
said Little Lion.

. . . Little Lion?